FEB 2 1 1996

Gracias, Rosa

MICHELLE MARKEL
Illustrated by DIANE PATERSON

ALBERT WHITMAN & COMPANY · Morton Grove, Illinois

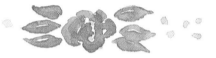

Library of Congress Cataloging-in-Publication Data

Markel, Michelle.
Gracias, Rosa / written by Michelle Markel;
illustrated by Diane Paterson.
p.   cm.
Summary: At first, a young girl does not like her new
babysitter, Rosa, but after getting to know her and learning
some of her language and customs, she is sad when
Rosa returns to her family in Guatemala.
ISBN 0-8075-3024-7
1. Guatemalans—United States—Juvenile Fiction.
[1. Guatemalans—United States—Fiction.
2. Babysitters—Fiction.]
I. Paterson, Diane, ill. II. Title.
PZ7.M33945Gr   1995   94-25979
[E]—dc20   CIP   AC

The text of this book is set in Stone Informal.
The illustrations are rendered in watercolor.
Design by Susan B. Cohn.

*For my two daughters, Lana and Sascha, without whom
this would never have been written. M.M.*

For my husband, John. D.P.

The first time Rosa came to our house, I didn't even want to meet her. I wished Allison, my old babysitter, wasn't moving away. I didn't want a babysitter who talked in Spanish.

"Rosa will take care of you now," my mom said. "She's a very nice lady, and she already knows some English."

Rosa peeked around to where I was hiding behind my mom. She reached into her pocket and pulled out a cloth doll.

"Para ti," she said. "Es de Guatemala."

The cloth doll was different from my other dolls. She was soft and small. She had dark hair in one long braid, just like Rosa.

I came out from behind my mom. I took the doll and turned her around in my hands. Her skirt and blouse had pretty colored stripes.

"She feels real nice," I said to Rosa. "Thank you."

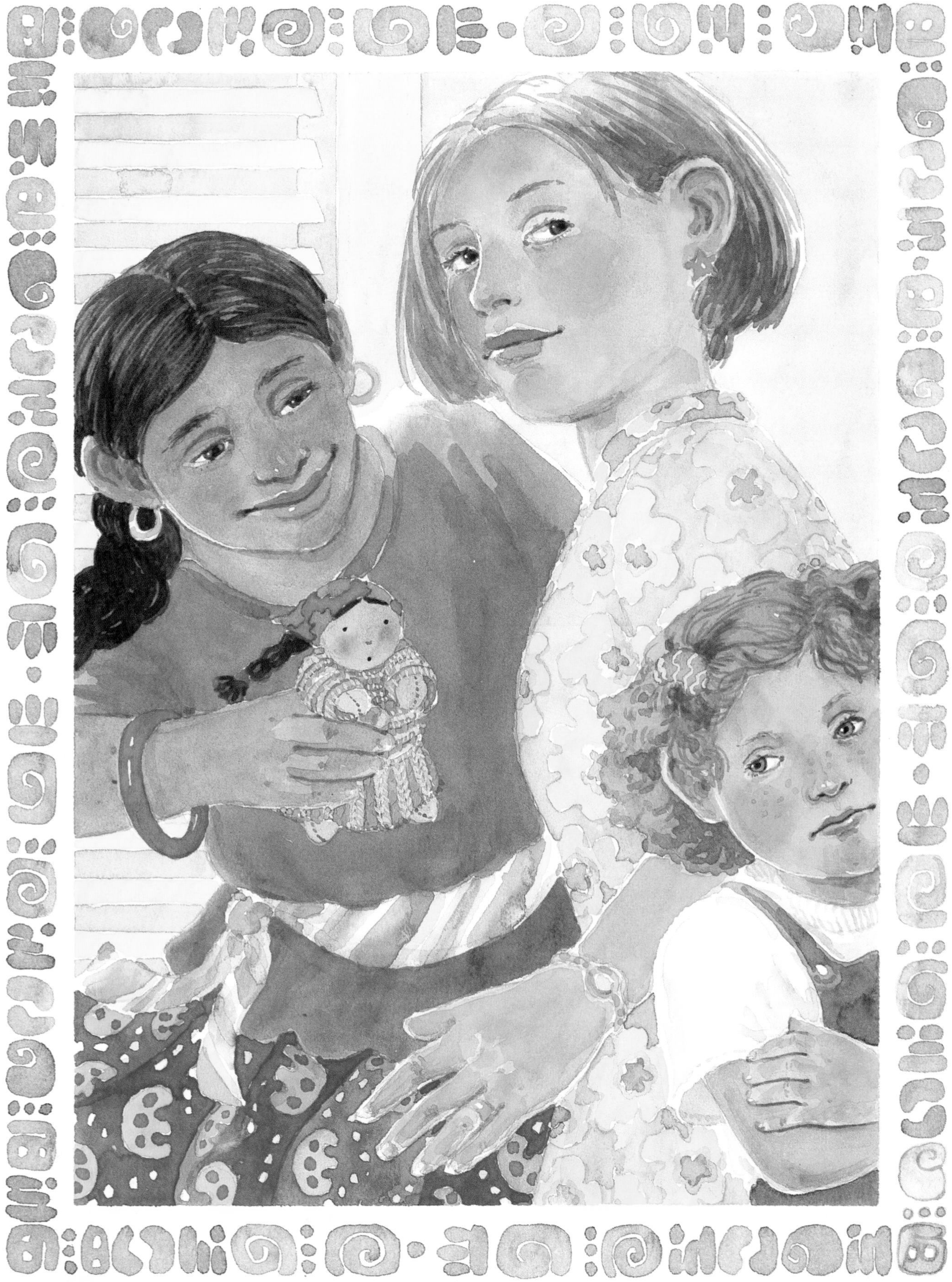

My mom told Rosa how to use the microwave and what to make me for lunch. My dad showed her how to play our videos and lock the house. We all showed her where my school was so Rosa would know where to pick me up each day.

"There it is!" I shouted.

"Katita's school," Rosa said. She called me Katita, but my real name is Kate.

As the weeks went by, Rosa learned more English. She started taking classes at night. At first all she could say were things like "My name is Rosa Arqueta" and "I live in Los Angeles." She learned more by shopping and watching TV and listening to songs on the radio. I taught her some words, too. We had fun playing together.

But Rosa always had her own way of doing things. One day I dressed up Jessica, my doll with wavy hair.

"My doll's going to the dance," I said. "What's your doll doing?"

Rosa took my cloth doll and walked her across the floor.

"She goes to the market."

"Doesn't she want to go to the dance?"

Rosa laughed.

"No, she can't go. She does not have vestidos de noche—fancy clothes. But she is happy. She sees the mountains, the flowers, and she hears many birds singing. At the market, she buys something sweet for her children."

Rosa often took me to the park after school. She liked talking with Inés and Marta, two other babysitters. One day, I made a cake in my bucket.

"Let's have a birthday party!" I said. "This is a banana chocolate vanilla cake."

Rosa scooped some wet sand and patted it into a little bun. Then she made another little bun.

"What are you making?" I asked.

"Tamales," she said. Inés and Marta laughed.

"Why are you making tamales?"

"Katita, in my country, we make tamales for children on el día de cumpleaños—the birthday. You want to help?"

We made lots of tamales. Rosa set each one in front of my cloth doll.

"Feliz cumpleaños," she said.

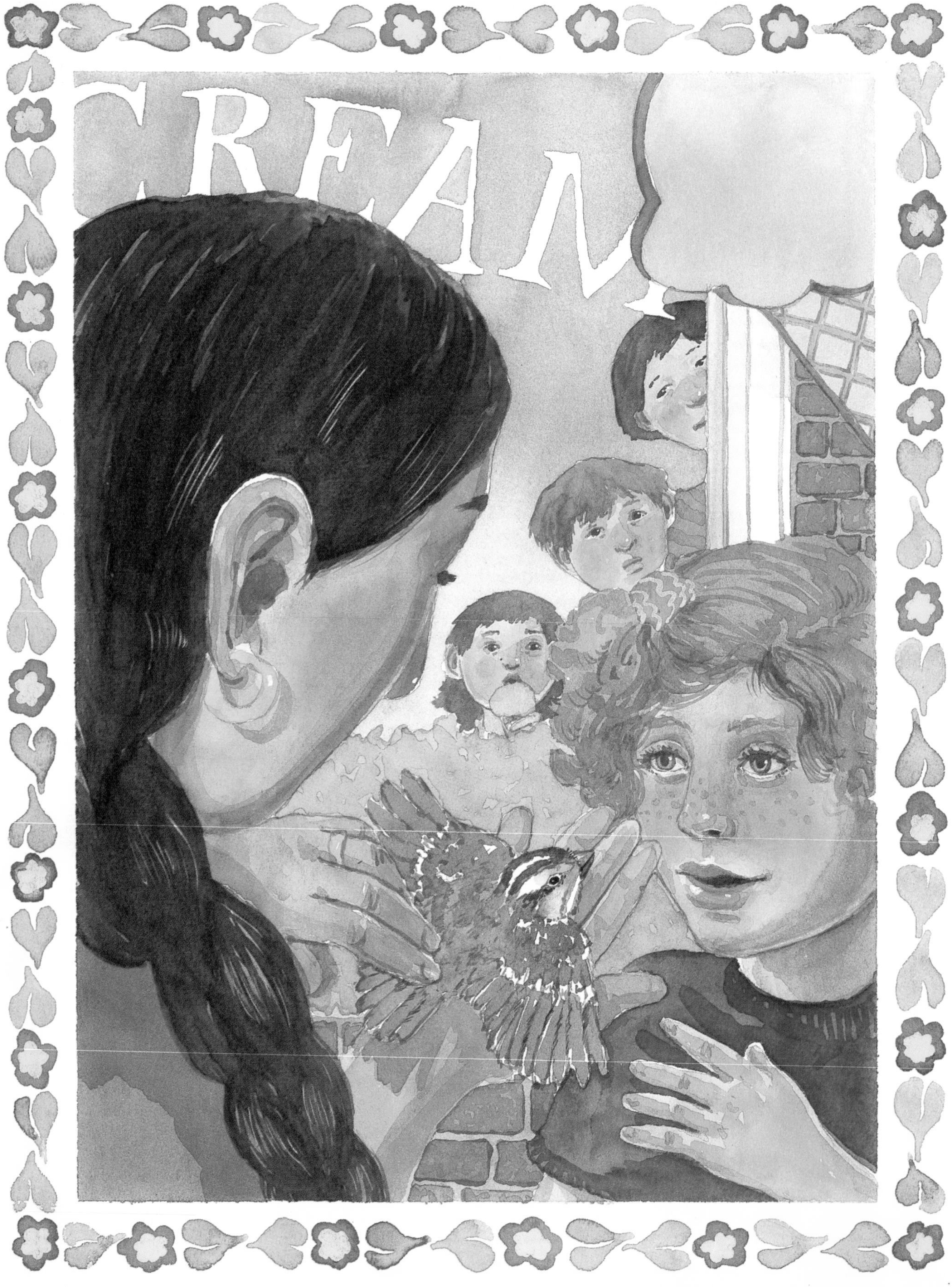

Once, on our way to the ice cream store, we saw a sparrow hit a window and fall to the ground. Rosa made a cradle for him with her hands. He was shaking. I knew he was really scared.

"Can we keep him, Rosa?" I asked.

"No, Katita," Rosa said. "Maybe el pájaro has children. He has to go home." Rosa stroked the bird's smooth brown feathers. She opened her hands, and the bird flew into the sky. I watched him go. I hadn't thought that bird might have a family.

One day I tore my favorite dress, the one with pink and purple hearts. When Rosa picked me up at school, I was crying.

"No te preocupes, mi amor," Rosa said, putting her arms around me. "When we get home, I fix the dress!"

"Did you ever have a dress you liked to wear over and over?" I asked Rosa when we got home. She was making quick, tiny stitches in my dress.

Rosa shook her head. "I never had fancy clothes like yours. I just had a few things. Where I come from, it is not a big city. It is like a farm."

"I'd like to live on a farm," I said. "Was it fun?"

Rosa laughed. "So much work! I don't know if you'd like it, Katita. You don't like to pick up your toys!

"There was no water, no electricidad. My mamá, she was always busy. She got up early as the sun to grind corn for tortillas. She had to walk to the well to get water. She had to go to the river to wash the clothes."

Rosa was quiet a moment. "But it was fun to feed los coches y las gallinas—the pigs and chickens. I felt important for my family. I also pulled weeds that grew near the corn. I watched the fields and scared the animals who came to eat our plants. I helped find wood for the fire."

"Did you ever get to play?" I asked.

"Sí. I had a little doll, made of cloth of many colors. I loved her very much. I had little clay dishes, and my mamá gave me a small piece of dough so I made my doll her own tortilla."

Rosa smoothed out the dress on her lap.

"¡Está terminado!" she said, holding it up to me.

The dress looked as good as new.

"¡Gracias, Rosa!" I said, and I kissed her cheek.

That night my mom and dad went to a party, so Rosa stayed late. We made tortillas to go with dinner. Then Rosa made pepián—chicken with onion, spices, and green peppers. I liked the way it tasted, except for the onions. I pushed them to the side of my plate.

Rosa watched me. She had tears in her eyes.

"What's wrong?" I asked.

"My Juana, she does the same thing. She does not like onions."

"Who's Juana?" I asked.

"My daughter. She's in Guatemala, with my mother."

"You never said you had a daughter!" I said. "How old is she? What's she like?"

"She's six. She's a pretty little girl. She likes to play games, like you."

"Why aren't you with her?"

Rosa bit her lip. "Katita," she said, stroking my hair, "where I come from, to live is hard. The beans and corns we grow, they don't bring us a lot of money. I came here because there are more jobs. Juana can't stay with her papá because sometimes he must leave for a long time to work somewhere else."

I thought for a minute. "Maybe Juana and her dad could visit you sometime," I said.

"Maybe," Rosa answered.

Rosa liked Los Angeles. "When I came here, it was like a dream," she said once. "So many stores, so many buildings, so many people from different countries!" There were things she'd never seen before, like big parks with fast rides and drinking fountains with icy water.

She said people in the United States were more free to say what they wanted and do what they wanted than people at home. "But here, everyone is always rushing, coming and going. In my country, we don't have many things, but life is more slow."

One thing we both liked to do was sing. Rosa sang songs she heard on the Spanish radio, and I sang songs from my favorite TV shows. Sometimes, when we played school, I sang to my dolls, or taught them rhymes like the one about the cat and the fiddle.

Rosa taught the dolls a poem about una pava— a little bird.

Por aquí pasó una pava.	A bird passed by here.
Muy chiquitita y voladora.	She was very little, and she was flying.
En su pico llevaba flores,	She was carrying flowers in her beak,
Y en sus alas mis amores.	And my feelings of love under her wings.

It was a nice poem. I drew a picture about it.

One day I heard my mom and Rosa talking in low voices in the kitchen. They talked for a long time.

I went to see if there was something wrong.

Rosa saw me standing in the doorway. She was holding a letter on the table.

"Katita, I work here and I send money to my family," she told me.

She looked at her letter.

"Now my Juana has food and clothes. But I miss her very much. I have to go to see her."

I imagined Juana, so far away from her mother.

I didn't want Rosa to go away, but I felt bad about Juana. I wanted her to be happy. So I got Jessica and brought her to Rosa.

When my mom saw what I was doing, she said, "You play with Jessica all the time. Are you sure you want to give her away? Maybe we could buy Juana something special."

"Jessica *is* very special! I know Juana will like her."

My mom thought about it. "Juana will like her, absolutely," she said.

Rosa and I hugged each other real tight.

"Gracias, Katita," Rosa said. "Eres muy amable."

Soon Rosa left for Guatemala. It was summer, so I
went to day camp. Camp was fun, but I missed Rosa.

My mom and dad helped me write her a letter:
"Dear Rosa. ¿Cómo estás? ¿Cómo está su familia? I'm
fine. I can count to one hundred and jump rope now.
When you come back, I'll show you. Te quiero, Kate."
("Te quiero" means "I love you" in Spanish.)

A month went by, and then another. One afternoon
we got a letter in a thin blue envelope. Inside was a
picture of Juana standing in front of some tall corn
plants. She was holding Jessica. Juana had dark hair
in one long braid, and she was smiling.

The letter said things were going better for Rosa's
family. Their crops had done well this year, and she
was going to stay.

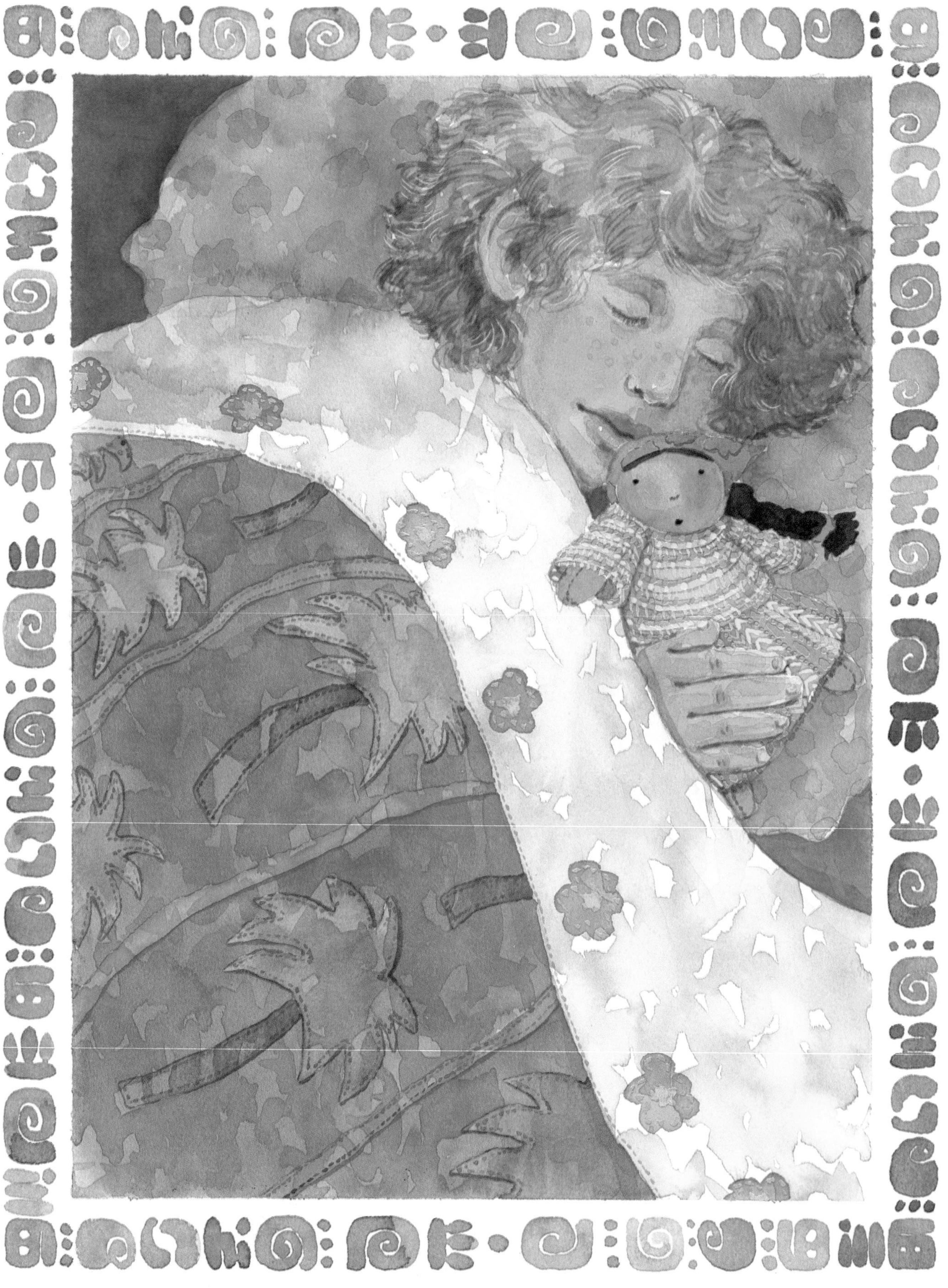

Now when I meet someone who speaks Spanish, I smile and say "Buenos días." I say a few words to Inés and Marta when I see them at the park. I'm in school all day, and in the after-school program, so I don't need a sitter anymore.

But I still have my cloth doll. Once in a while, I make her tamales for her birthday. Some nights I whisper to her about the pava. Sometimes I just hold her close to me. She's soft and small and has dark hair in one long braid, and I named her Rosa.

Glossary of Spanish Words

Guatemala is one of seven countries in Central America, a narrow area of land between Mexico and South America. Its ten million people include two main groups: Indians and Ladinos. The Indians live mostly in villages, speak one of several Indian languages, and follow a traditional Indian way of life. Ladinos speak Spanish and follow Spanish-American customs. They may be the descendants of Hispanic colonists and Indians or of pure Indian ancestry. Rosa is Ladina.

Buenos días: good morning
Coche: pig (Guatemalan word)
¿Cómo está su familia?: How's your family?
¿Cómo estás?: How are you?
Día de cumpleaños: birthday
Electricidad: electricity
Eres muy amable: You're very kind.
Es de Guatemala: It's from Guatemala.
Está terminado: It's finished.
Feliz cumpleaños: happy birthday
Gallina: hen
Gracias: thank you
Mamá: mother
No te preocupes, mi amor: Don't worry, my love.
Pájaro: bird
Papá: father
Para ti: for you
Pava: a colorful Guatemalan bird; a female turkey
Pepián: a Guatemalan dish made with chicken, peppers, onions, and spices
Sí: yes
Tamal (plural—tamales): chopped meat wrapped in cornmeal dough and steamed in corn husks
Te quiero: I love you.
Tortilla: a thin round pancake, usually made of cornmeal
Vestidos de noche: fancy clothes for going out at night